THE STORY KEEPERS

Episode 4

Ready, Aim, Fire!

Brian Brown and Andrew Melrose

CASSELL

Cassell

Wellington House, 125 Strand,
London WC2R 0BB

© Brian Brown and
Andrew Melrose, 1997

**Videos distributed by
S.P. Trust**

Triangle Business Park,
Wendover Road, Stoke
Mandeville, Nr. Aylesbury,
Bucks HP22 5BL
Tel. 01296 614430
Fax. 01296 614450

Designed by
Tony Cantale Graphics

First published 1997

**British Library Cataloguing-
in-Publication Data**
A catalogue record for this
book is available from the
British Library.

ISBN 0-304-33663-7

Printed in Spain by
Graficas Reunidas

Long ago, in the city of Rome,
there lived a mighty ruler.
His name was Nero.
He thought he was a god,
but the Christians knew he wasn't.
So Nero hated them.

One day there was a great fire.
Nero said the Christians started it,
and he sent his cruel soldiers after them.

Marcus, Justin and Anna
lost their parents during the fire.
Ben the baker and his wife, Helena,
took them into their home.
There, in a time of great danger,
they told the children stories about Jesus.

This book is about the adventures
of the Storykeepers.

"Cyrus, can you see the messenger yet?" asked Zak.
He was worried. He was waiting for his famous uncle,
Mordecai.

Cyrus and Anna were hiding in a tree.
They were on the lookout.
"Not a sign," replied Cyrus.
"Keep looking. But stay under cover."

Suddenly Anna spotted a
man. He was being chased
by soldiers.
"Here he comes!" she called.
"Nihilus is going to catch
him!" Cyrus cried.
"I know what to do," Zak
said.

6

Zak put an arrow in his bow and aimed at some barrels on a cart. He fired, but he missed.
Ben grabbed a bow and fired. Bull's-eye! Oil spilled out of the barrels. The soldiers slipped and slid.
And Mordecai disappeared into the crowd.

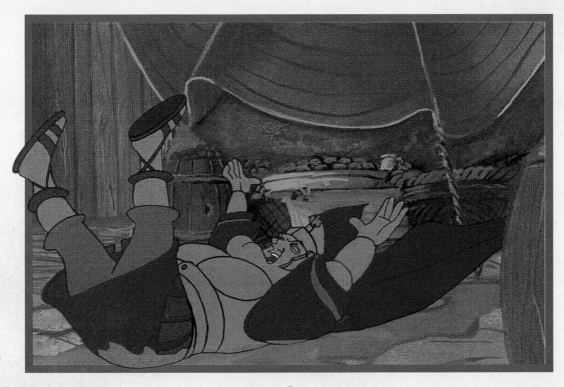

Nihilus shook his fist.
"I will get you Christians!" he
shouted. "You can't hide from me
forever!"

Back at the safe house, Ben and the children
greeted Mordecai. The children were excited to
see Zak's uncle because he was a famous soldier.
"Tell us about your adventures!" they said.
Zak pushed them away.
"He does not have time to tell stories," said Zak.
But Mordecai loved children. He told them a story
about Jesus and some children.

One day parents brought their children to Jesus
to be blessed.
But the disciples told them to go away.

Jesus said, "Let the boys and girls come to me. My kingdom belongs to people who are like them." No wonder the children all loved Jesus!

Zak was still unhappy.
He was ashamed that his
arrow had missed.
Ben said nothing. Nor did
Mordecai.
"I have something for
you, Zak," Mordecai said.
"It's a star of David from
your father."
Now Zak felt very proud.

At the palace, Nihilus reported back to Nero. He was still angry with the Christians.
"Let me destroy their houses, Caesar," he said. "I have a secret weapon that will shoot balls of fire at their homes."

Another soldier named Tacticus was a friend of Ben. He was worried when he heard about the plan. He told his servant, Darius, "We must warn Ben. He has a meeting tonight. Tell him that he is in danger."
Darius ran to find Ben.

At the meeting Ben told the Christians this story to make them brave:

Jesus and his disciples were going through the city of Jericho.
A blind man named Bartimaeus sat by the roadside calling out: "Son of David! Jesus! Help me!"

"Shh! Be quiet! Sit down!" The crowds shouted. But Jesus called the man to him.
"What do you want me to do for you?" he asked Bartimaeus.
"I want to see again," the man replied.

Jesus just looked at him, and Bartimaeus was able to see again. "Go home," said Jesus. "Your faith has made you see."

Darius burst into the room.
"There's going to be a fire!
The soldiers have a new weapon.
It shoots balls of flame!"
Suddenly a huge ball of fire dropped
from the sky. The house was set
alight.
Quickly, the gang put out
the flames.

"Tacticus will try to stop the bombing," said Darius.
"We cannot wait. We must escape," said Ben.
"Quickly, into the barrels," he ordered.
They did as Ben said. Justin and Darius rolled the barrels into a stream.
The Christians floated away past the soldiers.

Ben put Helena, Mordecai, Marcus, and Anna onto a
wagon.
"Justin and I will take my baker's wagon, Zak," he said.
"We'll meet you at the bakery."

Marcus and Anna were scared
by the fires.
"Why does Nero want to hurt us?"
they asked. "What have we done
wrong?"
Helena told them this story:

One day Jesus was in the synagogue,
the Jewish meeting house.
It was Sabbath, the day Jews are supposed
to do no work.

A man with a paralyzed hand was there.
The people watched Jesus. Would Jesus heal the man on the Sabbath?
"What is the right thing to do on the Sabbath?" Jesus asked. "To make someone better or let him die?"

"Stretch out your hand," Jesus said to the man.
And Jesus healed him.

Helena looked at the children.
"Sometimes you have to do what is right even if it gets you into trouble," she said.

Suddenly their horse reared in fright.
She bolted past Ben and Justin's wagon.
Zak couldn't control her. They were
heading directly into the fires!

Ben and Justin raced after them.
They caught up to the wagon.
"Jump!" called Ben to Helena.
She and the children jumped to safety
just in time.

But fires still blocked
their way.
"We're trapped!"
Justin cried.

"I have an idea," Zak said. "Cyrus, climb that statue and tie this rope on it. We'll fire the statue and knock a hole in the waterway."

Wham! Bull's-eye!
Water poured out
of the wall.

"You
did it, Zak,
you did it!"
Cyrus cried.
"Good shot!"
Mordecai said. "Your
father would be proud, Zak."

Thanks to Zak's idea, the fires were put out.
And all of the gang escaped.

THE STORY KEEPERS

There are thirteen exciting books
in The Storykeepers series.

Episodes 10–13
Join Ben and the gang for more
narrow escapes as they fight to keep
the stories of Jesus alive!